THE CAMPING TRIP

SCARPIA FOREST

RAJVEER JAIN

Copyright © Rajveer Jain
All Rights Reserved.

This book has been self-published with all reasonable efforts taken to make the material error-free by the author. No part of this book shall be used, reproduced in any manner whatsoever without written permission from the author, except in the case of brief quotations embodied in critical articles and reviews.

The Author of this book is solely responsible and liable for its content including but not limited to the views, representations, descriptions, statements, information, opinions and references ["Content"]. The Content of this book shall not constitute or be construed or deemed to reflect the opinion or expression of the Publisher or Editor. Neither the Publisher nor Editor endorse or approve the Content of this book or guarantee the reliability, accuracy or completeness of the Content published herein and do not make any representations or warranties of any kind, express or implied, including but not limited to the implied warranties of merchantability, fitness for a particular purpose. The Publisher and Editor shall not be liable whatsoever for any errors, omissions, whether such errors or omissions result from negligence, accident, or any other cause or claims for loss or damages of any kind, including without limitation, indirect or consequential loss or damage arising out of use, inability to use, or about the reliability, accuracy or sufficiency of the information contained in this book.

Made with ♥ on the Notion Press Platform
www.notionpress.com

Contents

I

THE FIELD TRIP

There lived four best friends Zayden White, Alex Johnson, Kenji Martin, and Katie Carver in Dallas, Texas.

After school, they used to play tennis.

Their school was organizing a field trip to the Scarpia Forest. All four friends went for the field trip.

They went in the school bus, and everyone in the bus was overly excited for the trip. It was 10:00 p.m., the bus tyre got punctured on a very dark and deserted road.

All the children in the bus were petrified and then Kenji saw a large shadow behind the bushes. After looking at that shadow, Kenji was scared and started sweating but he did not tell anyone about this.

When Katie saw him, she asked him *"Kenji, are you not feeling well?"* Then, Kenji replied *"No Katie, I -I -I -I a... a....m okay"*.

Kenji was trembling very badly.

They reached the Scarpia forest in the morning.

Everyone started to set up their tent. Zayden, Alex, and Katie started setting up the tents, but Kenji was still scared of the large shadow he saw behind the bushes last night.

Katie was sure that something is wrong with him.

When all the children settled their tents, everyone went for adventure in the forest with a forest guide.

They saw many eye-catching waterfalls and the river.

When all the children went to collect wood for the campfire, Zayden saw a restricted area of the forest where he saw a barbed wire fence.

He became curious about the restricted place.

At night, Zayden was still thinking of the restricted area. At the same moment, he heard loud screams which woke up everyone in the camp. After hearing the screams, Alex, Kenji, and Katie got very spooked out, especially Kenji.

Zayden was the only one who was not scared, he wanted to know who it was, but he did not want to take any risk.

The next morning, Zayden went to the restricted area alone to check again. When he reached the restricted area, he ignored the '*danger*' board and got inside.

It was very dark inside and he found a paper, it wrote '*open*'. He went back to the camp and told them about the restricted area and the paper he found there.

Alex, Kenji, and Katie were shocked when they heard that from Zayden.

The next morning, one boy was missing from the camp. Everyone was trying to find him in the camp. Zayden went to the restricted area to see whether he went inside or not, he saw a cavernous reflection, so he went closer, it was unbelievable what he saw.

It was a six and a half feet guy with sharp teeth and whitish-cream face!!

Zayden quickly came out of the restricted area and went to the camp. He told Alex, Kenji and Katie about it, and Kenji thought that he might be the same guy he saw in the bushes!

At midnight, everyone heard the same scream they heard the previous night.

When the screaming stopped, Zayden thought that he might be the same tall guy of the restricted area.

When everyone went back to sleep, Kenji went to answer nature's call in the bushes. When he was coming back, he saw someone who was walking around.

Kenji went closer to see who it was, he saw that it was the same tall guy!!! The tall guy kidnapped Kenji and took him to the restricted area.

Kenji started shouting *"Somebody help!"*.

Everyone was in deep slumber, so no one heard his voice. The next morning, they realized that Kenji was also missing. Then Zayden, Alex, and Katie, all three went to find him.

Zayden was sure that he was in the restricted area.

They went very deep in there. Alex found a paper, where there was a word written *'the'*.

Then Alex told Zayden and Katie about it. Zayden also had the paper with the word *'open'*.

They made the sentence *"open the."* They wanted to know what they had to open. The mystery was getting complicated.

They went further to find any other things which can be useful in solving the mystery. Then, Alex found a key with the inscription *"tree key."*

They didn't know the tree where they could use the tree key. They went on further and found numerous trees.

They figured out that it must be one of them but after looking around for a couple of hours, Katie saw a tree which had a golden glowing branch, which was weird. They thought that it must be the same tree, but they did not know how to unlock the tree with the key.

Zayden took a step back and then the floor where he stepped back fell so Zayden, Alex and Katie also fell with the floor.

They realised that there was an underground base, and they found a big golden box in there. When they picked up the box, they heard a scream which meant that the tall guy was close to the restricted area.

They knew that the tall guy lived in the restricted area!!!

The scream of the tall guy was coming closer and closer which meant that he was coming to the base!!!

They hid behind a wall, and just then, the tall guy came inside the base. Zayden, Alex and Katie were shocked when they saw him.

He was wearing a white coat, and he had a pristine white and creepy face!!! He took the mystery box with him and went back up. They slowly followed the guy.

The tall guy was going into a nearby graveyard. When they entered the graveyard, they saw that he took out a bottle full of smoky stones from the box. They waited for the tall guy to leave from there and once they were sure that the tall guy had left, they came out from hiding to find out more.

II

THE MYSTERY BOX

Zayden, Alex, and Katie found something which was unbelievable. They found extremely smoky stones that blinded them, and they were not able to open their eyes.

Alex opened his eyes, and he quickly opened the bottle.

As he opened the bottle, the smoke started oozing out and was spreading everywhere and something started happening to Alex!!!

He was getting bigger and taller like the same tall guy. Zayden and Katie did not see anything as it got very foggy.

Alex went to the camp to scream just like the tall guy.

Zayden and Katie did not understand anything as everything happened extremely fast. They went to find Alex.

Katie went further in the woods she found a map which showed the way of an island in which, a box of treasure was hidden.

She immediately went to tell Zayden about this. Zayden told her *"We will start the mission tomorrow early morning."* But Katie was still pondering about Alex and Kenji.

But Zayden tried to explain her *"they will be fine,* and *we will find them too"* but they did not know that Alex had become the same as the tall guy, as it was smoky, so Alex left, and Zayden and Katie didn't notice.

Only Kenji was in the barrier, all the children left the Scarpia forest except Charles Lunas and Robbin Parkwood.

Zayden wanted to involve both in the mission so that it can be easily accomplished, as Charles was an excellent spy, and Robbin was good at reading difficult things like maps and code languages.

It was the first flush of the morning, they packed their bag and carried the tents so that at night, they can sleep peacefully, and they also carried an underground metal detector which will help them to find mysterious things under the ground.

When they started moving ahead in the restricted area, Robbin saw three tall guys who jump scared him and Zayden and Katie noticed that one of the tall guys was the same one who used to scream in the midnight and the rest two were looking like Alex and Kenji!

They knew it that Alex and Kenji also turned into the same tall guy, and they will infect everyone. They decided to face that issue afterwards.

They ran as fast as they could and when they stopped, they found the same tree which was the base of the tall guy. When they went inside, they found the mystery box.

Charles saw a golden tag on the mystery box in which it was in scripted *'Brawl'.*

They opened the mystery box, it was empty!

They thought that the tall guy took all things from the box, or nothing existed in the box except the bottle, they were not sure.

They went ahead and found the same graveyard where they found the bottle of smoky stones. They entered the graveyard; and found the bottle of smoky stones.

Katie said *"Guys, we should not open the bottle because when Alex had opened the bottle, he got missing".*

They took the bottle and went back but, on the way, Charles found the same golden tag which was on the mystery box which meant that someone had taken the mystery box.

When they went further, the underground metal detector started beeping, which meant that something was underground.

They started digging and found the same mystery box.

When they opened the box, they found a small cell in it. They were very confused. But then Zayden also found a map of a secret chamber.

The chamber was a bit far from where they were standing. The map was starting from the graveyard. They also carried the bottle of smoky stones and the cell too.

When they started moving ahead, they found a cave with four different paths to choose, Zayden chose the first one, Katie chose the second one, Charles chose the third one, and Robbin chose the fourth one.

Zayden's path had a large dragon, and he found it unbelievable that there was a large dragon in there!!!

Zayden ran ahead and entered a small hole where the dragon will not be able to fit inside. The hole was very dark from inside and when he exited the place, and he noticed that it was the graveyard!!!

Katie's path had a water pipeline, she kept moving ahead but she by mistake touched the pipe, and then drops of water started leaking from the pipe.

Katie tried to fix it, but she shifted the pipe and suddenly, a lot of water started to leak, and Katie was stuck there as the water was leaking extremely fast and she started drowning in the water!!!

Charles's path had a large maze, he continuously kept moving ahead, he did not know where he was going but he found a key and a structure of the maze, when he memorized it, he easily escaped the maze, and he was teleported to the camp again.

Robbin's path had a bedroom!!!

He discovered a large bed, a large table, and the photo of a family. He exited back and tried to figure it out, he came back out of his path.

When everyone kept moving ahead, the three boys found each other but no one had any clue about Katie.

After some time, they heard noises from below the ground and suddenly the ground below them shifted and water came up on the ground.

They were very confused.

III
THE BARRIER

After the water was gone, they found Katie!

Katie had also escaped from the water. Then Robbin showed everyone the photo he found in that bedroom. Everyone was shocked to see that in the picture, one guy was as tall as the tall guy.

Charles saw something which was glowing in the corner of the frame, he touched the glowing portion of the frame.

The picture inside the frame automatically came out and the frame and showed another map which revealed the location of one more place.

When they reached that place after walking many miles, it was very difficult to believe that they found Alex and Kenji in a large barrier.

Zayden asked them *"How did you both get caught in the barrier"*. Then Kenji answered, *"When we were kidnapped by the tall guy, we got unconscious and when we opened our eyes, we found ourselves in this barrier".*

Then Katie asked them *"Then the other tall guys whose faces were like Alex and Kenji, who were they?"*

Alex answered "They are our duplicates and are controlled by a computer. They are robotic, and they were created by the tall guy.

First, they had to figure out how to make Alex and Kenji come out of the barrier. Kenji said, *"In the tall guy's graveyard, there is a computer from which he controls the barrier".*

They went back to the graveyard but in between, they found the tall guy. They tried to face him, but were afraid so they ran away, but then Charles got missing!!!

Charles was also caught by the tall guy. Everyone followed the tall guy to know what he was doing with Charles.

They kept following him and when they reached the place, it was a magical gate!!!

They entered the gate, and it was a whole different world, it was a very spectacular and gorgeous place.

The tall guy entered a place which was like a house. When they entered inside that place, there found the duplicates of the people who were in the barrier.

They returned to the barrier and told Alex and Kenji everything about the door and the secret world.

They were terrified to hear it. The next morning, Zayden, Katie and Robbin were walking ahead to the magical gate, but then Charles discovered some footprints behind the gate.

They went forward following the footprints. When they reached the destination, that place was a treehouse.

They climbed the weird treehouse and entered in, but they were terrified to see that the tall guy was in the treehouse, and he saw them and tried to catch them!!!

When Robbin was almost caught by him, he showed the tall guy's family photo he found on the bedroom-like place of the large rock.

When the tall guy saw the photo, he got back his senses and realised everything.

Then Zayden asked, *"who are you?"*.

Then the tall guy answered, *"My name is Germen Roberton, and I am from New York. I came to the Scarpia forest with my family for camping, and we all went to collect sticks for the campfire. There I saw a green coloured ball, and then I picked up the ball and rest all I don't remember."*

Then Katie asked, *"Do you know where you found the ball?"*.

Then he answered, *"I just remember that a school bus was passing by."* All three of them were very amazed to hear it from him.

Then Robbin said, *"now can you unlock the people who are trapped in the barrier".*

Then Germen's mouth got unglued and answered, *"I am so sorry guys, I control the barrier with a computer which needs a cell that is in the mystery box, but I forgot where I placed the box".*

Then Zayden realised *"Guys, I took the cell out from the box and gave it to Katie".*

Then Katie said *"but I handed over the cells to Robbin".*

Then Robbin answered, *"I handed over the cells to Charles".*

Charles was in the barrier, everyone sprinted to the barrier and asked Charles to hand over the box to them, when Charles was passing the box to Katie, they both got a very bad current from the barrier.

Then Germen explained *"this barrier is protected by laser that is why, you can't touch the barrier".*

They were stuck in between the mystery, but then Germen suddenly remembered and cheerfully said, *"guys, I can remove anything from the barrier with the help of my tablet and it can work without the cell".*

Everyone entered the magical door rapidly and ran towards the tablet, but they were thunderstruck to see that the tablet was hacked!!!

But Robbin was very good at hacking, so they left that to Robbin.

Then they were left with only one task which was to find the green ball. But then Germen told them that *"guys, listen to me carefully, the green ball is very strong, and it can infect anyone".*

For their safety, he gave them two pairs of gloves so that they don't get infected by the ball.

The next morning, they went to the magical door and got teleported to a random place where they found thousands of green balls!!!

They reached the place in a New York minute; it was a gut churning moment!!!

When they were moving ahead, the green balls were following them, but they didn't notice. When Katie moved back, the green ball was about to jump scare, then, Robbin caught the ball in a cloth and saved them.

IV
GREEN BALL

When Robbin saved both Zayden and Katie, suddenly, a green ball swooped down on Robbin's head! Robbin got infected by the ball!!!

And he became tall and evil as Germen was before. Then, Robbin started chasing them.

They split in three different ways; Robbin was confused about who had entered which way.

He went in a random way. But he entered Germen's path. When Germen saw him sprinting towards him, he kept running and running and running!!!

Germen hid behind a rock; and Robbin went in the other direction.

Katie was relaxing under a tree as her legs were twinging. When she saw Robbin following her, she started running but was very tired and that's why she couldn't run fast.

After a while she climbed on a tree and Robbin ran towards another path.

While Zayden was wandering and lost his way, but when he moved back, he noticed that Robbin was running towards him. He quickly started running on the same path. Katie and Germen were also running.

All three of them were being chased by Robbin.

Then they stopped in their track, and saw that Kenji and Alex got infected by the green balls which had reached the barrier by now. They were in a big danger!!!

Kenji, Alex, Charles and Robbin were about to attack them but then a stranger came to rescue them.

They were surprised to see that they were safe and thanked the person who saved them. Then, Germen went behind a tree so that the stranger doesn't see his creepy face.

Then Katie asked him *"what's your name?"*.

The person answered *"My name is Walter Hugo, and I am here to explore new places. I always wanted to become an explorer and to start my career, I came to Scarpia forest with my father, but one midnight, me and my father were sleeping in different tents, and I heard some screaming from outside and saw a large shadow! I tried to sneak out, when I saw a tall guy who entered my father's tent and kidnapped him!"*.

When Germen heard that from Walter, he revealed himself. When Walter saw him, he ran away quick as he knew that he was the tall guy who kidnapped his father!

But then, Zayden and Katie explained him everything that he is not at all evil now.

After hearing this from them, Walter started arguing with Germen about that moment. Germen was very sorry for his actions.

Then Katie asked Walter *"where are the other tall guys who were attacking us?"*.

Then Walter said, *"they all were teleported to the barrier"*. Then Zayden said, *"Do you have any idea that how to unlock the people who are stuck in the barrier?"*

Walter told them about a mystery by which they can unlock them from the barrier, he told that "there is a secret place in a large waterfall which is located in the outskirts of Texas".

When they started their journey, their global positioning system (GPS) was telling them to cross a large wooden bridge which was very weak and ninety-two feet high! They were very scared to cross the bridge, and when they stepped on it, in between, one piece of wood fell into the water!

Then Zayden said, *"On the count of three, we will sprint towards the end, one......two......three!"* One by one they all started sprinting but in between, Walter was about to fall! He was hanging on the bridge; his hand was sweating very badly and was about to slip.

Then Zayden hurriedly came to hold his hand, but Zayden could not balance himself and was about to fall. Then Germen reached them to help but he was not able to pull them up but then, they all fell as they both were very heavy and even Katie fell with them, as the bridge broke down.

When they landed in the water, Walter saw something besides a rock, and when they went ahead, they witnessed the waterfall!

When they went closer to the waterfall, they saw something behind it, they discovered a cave!!!

They entered the cave and found some chemical drums. Then Germen noticed that there are a pair of reading glasses on the floor, and when Germen wore it, he saw some lasers, which meant that the lasers were invisible and the glasses infrared!

When they crossed the lasers, they picked up the chemicals and went back. When they brought the chemicals back with them, Walter tried to mix 2-3 chemicals.

But by mistake, Walter spilled the chemical on his feet, and got teleported to the barrier, but Zayden, Katie and Germen did not know where he was teleported!!!

They tried to find Walter for several hours, and eventually found him at the barrier. They were surprised that the chemicals had teleported him to the barrier!

V

THE CHEMICALS

They were very confused and puzzled to see that the chemicals had teleported Walter to the barrier!

Katie asked, *"how did this happen?"*.

Then Zayden said *"Katie, remember in our chemistry class we studied that mixing 2-3 chemicals together at a time can sometimes be dangerous." Katie said, "yes I remember, and it's our fault!"*.

At that time, Germen remembered something, *"Oh, guys I have an extra chemical which can unlock them when they drink it"*.

Zayden and Germen went to the graveyard to find out the chemicals while, Katie went to find Walter. But while wandering, Katie spotted someone. She went closer to see who it was.

She went closer and closer; when she found a small boy who was sobbing.

Katie asked him *"who are you and what are you doing here?"*

The boy answered, *"my name is Tyler Roberton, and I came here with my family for camping, but one day, I discovered a green ball in the bushes, I went forward to look at it, but from the other side, my father took it but then, the green ball exploded, and my father vanished, from that day I'm trying to find them."*

While, Zayden and Germen were in the graveyard, trying to find the chemicals.

Germen found a chemical in a corner, but before they stepped out of the graveyard, Katie reached the graveyard with Tyler.

Germen and Tyler were surprised and happy to finally see each other! They hugged each other tightly. Zayden's mind was puzzled, but Katie explained him that Germen was Tyler's father.

Germen asked Tyler *"how did you survive the explosion that day?"*. Tyler answered, *"I don't remember how I survived, and I don't know where our family is."*

Then Katie said, *"We will help you find your family, but first, we need to open the barrier"*.

Tyler shockingly answered *"What! while wandering, I discovered a remote in the graveyard and, when I went closer to it, I saw that it was written 'barrier' on it"*.

They all directly sprinted to the graveyard. But the remote was not there! They tried to find it.

They searched the whole graveyard, but they didn't find it anywhere. They went back but while walking, a green ball jump scared them by jumping in front of them!

They started running and kept running and running!

They found a cottage in between so they entered the cottage in a whiff. It was dark and pitch-black inside. When they turned on the light inside, they found the remote!!!

It was a miracle that they found that remote in the cottage! They immediately went to the barrier and tried to unlock it.

When Germen was about to press the button of the remote, suddenly, the remote slipped from his hands and broke down!!!

They were extremely shocked to see that the remote broke down in the last second!

They had a golden chance to finally open the barrier. Kenji and Alex in the barrier got glum.

But Katie was shocked to see Walter in the barrier!

She asked him "*Walter, how did you reach the barrier?*".

Walter answered, "*When the chemicals got spilled on my feet, I got teleported to the barrier*".

Katie answered, "*Thank god, you are okay, we were very worried about you*".

They tried to find another solution. Then Germen realized another secret place!

Germen told everyone about another place where he used to live *"Guys, I have another secret place where I used to live in the woods"*.

Germen took everyone with him. He went in the same cave where they had four paths. Zayden and Katie were surprised to see that it is the same place they found on their mission!

Germen took them in one of the paths. That path had a bedroom.

Zayden remembered something *"Katie, remember Robbin was telling us that his path had a bedroom"*.

"Yes, I remember," said Katie.

Germen screamed very loudly as if he got a heart attack!

Tyler asked him *"Dad, why did you shout so loudly?"*

Germen answered, *"Our family photo is missing!"*

Zayden remembered that Robbin showed them the family photo of Germen. He quickly went to the barrier and asked Robbin *"Robbin, I want Germen's family photo"*.

Robbin asked Zayden *"But, why do you want his family photo?"*.

Zayden answered, *"It is a very long story, I will tell you afterwards but please give me the family photo."*

VI

THE FAMILY PHOTO

Zayden quickly sprinted to the cave with the family photo and gave it to Germen. Germen was on cloud-nine when he saw the family photo. Everyone was confused to see why Germen was extremely glad to see the photo.

Germen touched a part of the photo, then the photo turned into the other side, and it unlocked a keycard. Everyone was astonished to see that a keycard was hidden in a frame!!!

Everyone again went to the barrier and tried to open it through the keycard, but it was not opening. Then Germen spotted a riddle written on it *"I am a shiny green stone found near a river"*.

Every one of them was baffled after reading it.

Zayden got the answer *"Yes, Its Emerald!"*.

Then, Katie said *"But we don't know which river it is talking about"*.

They tried to search for the river, it was very difficult for them to find the river. They again tried to figure out the riddle.

The next morning, they went to find the river. They went ahead but, when they were passing through the barrier, they noticed that the barrier was empty!

They were very worried that where did they go! They tried to find them.

They didn't find anyone. At that point of time, Germen noticed that the remote was still left there.

By looking at the remote, Germen realized and told everyone that *"Guys, I had fixed a button which can control the ground of the barrier"*.

So, when the remote slipped from his hands, the button broke and after some time, the ground got opened, that means they are in my underground chamber.

Germen started blaming himself *"This is all my mistake; I broke the remote"*.

Tyler answered, *"No dad, it's not your mistake"*.

Then Katie asked Germen *"Germen, do you remember what all you keep there?"*.

Germen answered her *"I keep my weapons there, so that when I go out, I carry one of them with me"*.

They all went to the barrier; and noticed that the ground of the barrier had disappeared!

"How will we reach your underground chamber; we cannot go to the barrier?" said Zayden.

Germen told everybody about another way to go in the chamber. Everyone followed Germen, where he was taking everyone was a whole new place for them. They reached a pond.

Germen said *"We must hop in the pond"* but it was very deep! That made Zayden's jaw drop as he was petrified of water.

He was unable to hop in but, he started thinking that in school also he was not able to dive in the pool, everyone used to browbeat him but now, he encouraged himself that he can dive in.

Then he closed his eyes and dived in without being scared.

When he opened his eyes, he noticed that he was able to swim, he was very glad to see this.

"But take care because the pond is extremely deep," said Germen. Everyone was very shocked that the pond is extremely deep and a secret place to the chamber.

Then, Germen told them *"Now, first we will go underground and then in the end, you will find a vent. The vent may be closed so; to open the vent, I will give you a screwdriver and an oxygen mask to breathe in water"*.

Germen gave them a screwdriver to open the vent in there.

They all went deeper in the pond except Germen. Germen was spectating them from the cameras in the vent, but he didn't tell anyone that the vent also had CCTV cameras.

When they reached the vent, the screwdriver was in Katie's hand. She was about to open the vent, but the screwdriver accidently slipped from her hand and slid away further into the depth!!!

They started to panic!

Katie started saying *"I am so sorry guys, it slipped from my hand"*.

Then, Tyler asked them *"Now what should we do! We don't have the screwdriver"*.

Then Zayden said, *"We should go further, we might find something new"*.

They went further and further. They were finding it difficult to breathe despite the oxygen masks, as they were in the water for so much time and there was no option for them to go.

VII

THE CHAMBER

They were moving nonstop... and finally reached the end. They were extremely amazed to see that they found a treasure chest at the end. While Germen was worried that why they hadn't reach the vent till now!!!

Then, Germen decided to jump in the pond. When he reached there, he opened the vent with a Swiss pen knife.

In the vent, he kept moving and moving and at the end, he discovered a magical door. The magical door pushed germen in it and teleported him in the barrier and he fell in the chamber.

While Zayden, Katie and Tyler ignored the treasure chest and first tried to complete their task. When they were returning towards the vent, Tyler discovered that the vent was open!

Tyler asked them *"Guys, should we go inside, I think someone is in the vent"*.

Zayden answered, *"No Tyler, first we should go up and tell Germen about the treasure".*

Tyler didn't listen to them and went inside the vent.

Zayden and Katie ignored Tyler and went out of the pond but, they didn't know that Germen had gone in the vent and was teleported to the barrier. Tyler also discovered the magical door, and he was also pushed in.

While Zayden and Katie reached out of the pond, they noticed that Germen was not there!

They tried to find Germen everywhere, but they didn't find him. They were very worried about him. They again jumped in the pond and went in the vent.

In the vent, they didn't find anything even the magical door had disappeared! They didn't know that there was a magical door, and they didn't know where Tyler was.

Zayden and Katie came out of the pond. After coming out, they spotted a laptop which showed the feed of the CCTV camera of the vent!!!

Then, they knew that Germen was spectating them from it!

When they played the previous recording of the camera, they saw that Germen had gone in the vent and a magical door was also there which teleported them somewhere and after some time, Tyler went in the magical door and got teleported somewhere!!!

Their mind was very puzzled that how come the magical door suddenly disappeared at that point of time!

They went back in the vent to check that how did the magical door disappear. When they reached the vent, the magical door was not there but found a dead end.

They had no way to go but, they discovered a pint-sized button!

When they pressed the button, the dead end of the vent opened! They went inside, the place was very grimy and dirty. They were moving ahead but, in between, they found a map which showed the directions of a river!!!

They thought it was the river asked in the riddle. They hopped out of the vent and tried to figure out the map.

When they started moving forward, they observed an open sewer from which, a green light was emitting!

They went inside the sewer and noticed that a torch was lying on the floor.

Zayden said, *"I think something is fishy because at one point of time, Germen and Tyler got teleported somewhere from the magical door and when we came there, the magical door had disappeared and now we have found a torch in an open sewer"*.

Then Katie said *"Yes, it sure is fishy, we should go further, we might find something"*.

They carried the torch with them and went further. After moving further, they found a torch with pink light.

They were very confused. They also carried the pink light with them, and when they went further, they reached a dead end!!!

Then they went to the other side of the sewer and found another torch with yellow coloured light!

They picked it up and dashed out of the sewer. They went out of the sewer.

Zayden said, *"That was very weird"*.

Then Katie said, *"Yes, but right now we should focus on searching Germen and Tyler"*.

It was evening, they were still trying to search for them.

Then Zayden realized *"Oh yes, the barrier, we forgot to see there"*.

Then Katie answered *"No, don't you remember, Germen told us that the ground of the barrier has disappeared, and everyone are at the chamber. We will find the entry of the barrier tomorrow but, right now we should sleep, it's very dark"*.

Then Zayden said *"Ok, let's go"*.

Next morning, they went to find the entry of the chamber. They were roaming around the whole Scarpia forest trying to figure out how will they enter the chamber.

Then, Katie got an idea, she told Zayden "We should go to the vent of the pond, we might find something new if we go further and further".

They again jumped in the pond and opened the vent with the screwdriver and headed inside the vent and started swimming forward.

After moving forward, they found a torch with blue light! They headed further, they found a torch with orange light and at the end, they picked up both the torches and went forward.

At the end, they found a small door, Zayden opened the door with the screwdriver.

After opening it, they fell somewhere and noticed that it was the sewer!

It was connected to the pond!

The water started leaking there and after some seconds, the water suddenly started leaking in a frenzy and it became a disaster for Zayden and Katie!!!

They started to sprint as fast as they can. Zayden spotted a ladder, he quickly placed the ladder and started climbing it.

They were about to come out, but water was coming with so much pressure that it was about to wash away the ladder but, somehow Zayden didn't let the ladder move away.

He was holding the exit of the sewer from one hand and from other hand he was holding the ladder and Katie was also saved as she was holding the bottom of the ladder.

After some time, the water stopped moving and they finally came out of the sewer.

They didn't have any idea about how to unlock the chamber and save them.

VIII
THE COFFEE SHOP

They didn't have any idea how to unlock the barrier so they ignored the barrier and first focused on the riddle so that they might find something to open the barrier.

Zayden said, *"A river was asked in the riddle"*.

Katie answered, *"Yes, but we don't know where the river is that they are talking about"*.

They continued their mission. They were starving badly as there was scarcity of food and water. They sat down under a tree but, they spotted something very far away.

They went closer to it, they discovered a coffee shop, they entered the shop. The shop was empty.

They went inside the kitchen and checked whether there was coffee or not.

They checked everywhere, but they didn't find anything. They again tried to search for something, but they didn't find anything. They were going out of the kitchen but finally, Zayden spotted something!!!

They went back to the kitchen and saw that there was a very small door! They needed to crawl to go inside.

They started crawling and went forward. It was a very long way. They finally came out after some time but, the place they were in was a bit weird.

The place was very small, there was just one hole and nothing else. They hopped in the hole.

The hole was very dangerous!

The hole was like a slide, it was extremely fast! The slide was unstoppable!!!

They finally reached down but, the place where they plunged was also weird like that, but it was bigger than the one before. The place was full of weapons!

They kept moving forward and forward, in between, Zayden saw someone!!!

Zayden and Katie followed him. After some time, that guy turned back, Zayden and Katie were very happy to see that guy because, that guy was Charles!!!

Zayden said, *"Nice to meet you Charles, after so much time"*.

Zayden and Katie finally met Alex, Kenji, Robbin, Germen, Tyler and Walter. They even had a kitchen in the chamber!

They both were surprised to see ample of food!

Katie asked them *"how did you guys find so much food?"*.

Kenji answered her *"Germen even had a kitchen in the chamber, he used to have his meal here"*.

Zayden and Katie first consumed something as they were famished.

After consuming some food, they explained the riddle to everyone. Everyone was ready to start the mission but, they didn't have any exit!!!

They were in the chamber for 2-3 hours trying to figure out how to get out.

After some time, Walter got an idea, he told everyone, *"Guys, we can dig from the wall, as it is soil, it would be easy to dig it"*. Everyone agreed on this.

Everyone took one shovel as they had some shovels in the chamber and started to dig it.

They kept digging and digging, they found a treasure box again. When they picked up the treasure box from its position, water started to come from there!!!

Zayden, Katie, Tyler and Germen knew that the water came from the pond. They told everyone that the water came from a pond. They kept the treasure box with them.

The water entered the chamber so they couldn't go up. They were stuck.

Zayden gave them an idea, he said "*We have only two ways to go up, we can do something and come out from the pond, or we can keep digging and digging and go up*".

Then Alex, Robbin, Tyler and Walter voted for going up from the path of the pond and Katie, Kenji, Charles and Germen voted for digging more.

It was a tie.

After that, they all started arguing about how they should go up.

IX

THE IMPOSSIBLE ESCAPE

Then, Zayden tried to stop them, but they weren't listening to him and kept fighting.

Charles got an idea, he told everyone *"Guys, we can do one thing, the people who voted for going up through the path of pond can try to go from there and people who voted for digging more can keep digging".*

Everyone agreed, the people who voted for going through the path of pond tried to figure out how to go up and the people who voted for digging more kept digging and digging.

Zayden was confused regarding what should he do because he was very confused about where should he work as he had supported both the options.

He decides to study the map of the Scarpia forest (which he had) and find which river is the riddle talking about.

Robbin got an idea for going up from the path of the pond, he told Alex, Tyler and Walter *"Guys, we can build stairs to go up and down".*

Alex refused him, *"No, we can't make stairs, it will take so much time. We should make a lift; we can control the lift with a rope".*

Tyler asked Alex *"Are you sure that the rope will be stable?".*

"Yes, Tyler it will be stable." Said Alex.

Alex brought a rope as they even had a rope. Alex, Robbin, Tyler and Walter were trying to make a lift. While Katie, Kenji, Charles and Germen were still digging, water started leaking again!!!

They tried to cover it so that the water doesn't leak because they didn't want to start a new disaster. When they were covering it, suddenly, water started coming out in a jiffy!!!

The water was unstoppable, after 15-20 minutes, when the water finally stopped, they noticed that the water came from a massive place!

Germen said *"Guys, I think this is the exit, we should go from here".*

Kenji refused him *"No we should not, it might be a trap".*

Everyone supported Germen, Kenji had to trust him.

When they were going there, Charles reminded them *"Guys, we should carry the weapons, we might face some problems further"*.

Kenji went to bring the weapons for everyone.

Zayden said "Guys, let me bring the map of the forest so that we can know the locations and all".

When they both went back to take their stuff, and were going back but, Kenji discovered a button!

When he pressed the button the entry of that place got closed as it also had a door, and no one knew about it!

Everyone was blank that how did it close.

Robbin said, "We should go find the exit now, when we go out from here, we will pick them up from there".

Zayden started scolding Kenji *"Why did you press the button?"*.

Kenji said, *"I am sorry Zayden, please forgive me"*.

Zayden answered, *"Okay, but how will we escape from here?"*.

Then Kenji got an idea *"Zayden, we can use Alex's idea of going up from a lift"*.

Zayden asked Kenji, *"Kenji, are you sure that we will be able to make a lift?"*.

Kenji answered him *"Yes Zayden, I'm sure we will be able to make a lift, we are always successful in whatever work we do and believe fully in".*

Zayden said, *"Yes, you are right, we can build a lift".*

They were ready to start the work. They needed some pieces of wood, one rope and a pulley.

They didn't have anything of these. They tried a frugal innovation, they had neither wood nor a pulley but, and the rope was with Alex, who was on the other side of the door.

They tried to observe their surroundings, they discovered a jute bag in there, they tried to open the jute from it and use it as a rope.

They took out the jute, but it was very challenging for them to bind the rope above.

Meanwhile, others were still moving, trying to find the exit, and after some time, they finally found the exit!

Everyone ran towards the exit, but Charles took a wrong step, and the floor disappeared, and a tightrope appeared and below the tightrope was lava!!!

Alex, Katie, Germen and Walter had already passed the tightrope as they were ahead when Charles took a wrong step and Charles, Robbin and Tyler were left behind.

Tyler went first, He kept walking and walking but, suddenly, his leg slipped!

He was falling but, Charles saved him in a jiffy.

Charles pulled Tyler up and both escaped but, Robbin was terrified of lava. Everyone encouraged him, then he got his confidence back.

He took his first step and was slowly moving forward but, by mistake he lost his balance.

He fell in the lava, and no one could help him!!!

X
THE CRYPTIC EXIT

Everyone was extremely terrified! Robbin fell in the lava! Everyone was trying to see if he was okay. No one could see him.

The others thought that he may not be alive, and they could do nothing to help him, they felt helpless, they ran away to save their own lives.

They were still feeling bad for Robbin. They kept sobbing for him.

When they exited that place, they came to a whole different world! It was like a grassland!

When Alex took his first step, he fell in a trap and when Charles took his next step he fell in a different trap! Just like this everyone fell in a trap!!!

The traps were like labyrinths. Everyone was moving aimlessly, but after some time, some of them met each other.

Alex and Charles found each other and Germen and Walter also found each other but, Katie and Tyler were alone in their traps and, they were still trying to find the way out.

Alex and Charles kept trying to find the way, and after some hours, they finally found a way out but, it was night, so they didn't see anything so, they fell in a river!!!

When they came out of the river, they discovered an unbelievable place.

They discovered a castle!

They entered the castle, and after entering the castle, suddenly many lights turned on!

The castle was very spectacular from inside. There was a red carpet to walk on and there was also a throne.

They were exploring all the rooms and, Charles discovered a sewer in the basement!

They knew that something is suspicious.

They were trying to open the sewer, but it was very tight. In their second attempt, they opened the sewer but, when they were looking into the sewer, they saw Zayden and Kenji on the ladder of the sewer!!!

In their second attempt, they could opened the sewer because Zayden was also pushing up from inside.

They were very happy to meet each other again.

Alex asked Zayden and Kenji *"how did you guys reach here from the sewer?".*

Then Zayden replied to him *"We were still in the chamber trying to make a lift but, we didn't have any stuff through which we can make a lift so, we started digging so, after some time we found a ladder, so, we started climbing it and through this ladder, we reached a sewer, in the sewer we found another ladder and through it, we reached here".*

Alex and Charles were amazed to hear this from Zayden.

Kenji asked them *"Where is everyone else?".*

Charles explained him everything that how did everyone scatter but, he didn't tell them that Robbin fell in the lava.

They were exploring the castle and trying to find new things.

When everyone came back to the main hall with empty hands, they heard some weird noises.

The noise was coming from the attic of the castle! When they went up to see, they found an old man with his hands, legs and face tied with rope!!!

They untied the rope, then Charles asked the old man *"Who are you and how did you come here?".*

The old man replied to him "I am Mark Hugo, and I came to the Scarpia forest with my son for camping because, my son always wanted to be an explorer. One night, I saw someone outside my tent. I ignored that, but the guy entered in the tent and kidnapped me, and my son was asleep as we were sleeping in different tents".

They were very puzzled because, Walter told them the same story. Tyler asked Mr. Mark *"What's your son's name?"*.

Mr. Mark replied to him *"His name is Walter; I don't know if he is okay or not"*.

Everyone was incredibly surprised to hear that from Mr. Mark!!!

They didn't tell Mr. Mark about Walter.

They had no idea what to do next, if Mr. Mark found out that Walter had been with them, he might start arguing with them.

Everyone went out of the castle.

XI
THE MASSIVE HALL

Everybody went out of the castle and tried to find everyone else. While moving in the forest, they found Katie!

Charles asked Katie *"How did you come out of the holes?"*.

Katie replied to him *"I just accidently found a way out of the holes, so I kept wandering here and there trying to find the others"*.

They kept moving to find Germen, Tyler and Walter.

After moving for long, they sat under a tree to take rest as it was midnight.

When they woke up in the morning, they saw some light coming from a tree.

First, they thought that it was the sunlight, but when they went close to it, they thought that it was a flashlight, and when they went closer to it, they knew that it was neither sunlight nor flashlight, it was a different light.

The light was coming from a massive hole in the tree.

They went inside the hole, at the end, they reached a large and empty hall. A small tree led to a massive hall!!!

The hall had so many gates, everyone was very confused.

Alex picked a door which took him to the hall again with a different door, then he picked a different door which took him to the hall too with another door.

After trying a few doors, a random door was opened, they tried to check that who was it, and they saw that it was Tyler!!!

They only needed to find Germen and Walter, but Mr. Mark didn't know that Walter was involved with them.

Everyone was trying to figure out how to find a door through which they can find a new path. After an hour, Zayden found an odd door which was of a different colour, size and look.

Everybody went in the odd door, that door did not take them back to the hall but, at the end, there was another magical door! They entered the magical door which teleported them to their camp.

At the camp they even found Germen and Walter! Everyone found each other and Mr. Mark and Walter were very happy to see each other.

Mr. Mark asked Walter *"You were involved with them, Walter?"*.

Walter replied, *"Yes dad, and thank you so much, guys for finding my father"*.

Tyler asked everyone *"Guys, where is Robbin?"*.

Tyler and Zayden didn't know that Robbin was dead. Everyone started sobbing when he said that.

Tyler and Zayden were confused.

Alex told them *"Robbin died!!!"*.

Zayden and Tyler were hysteric when they heard this. No one wanted to talk about that topic anymore.

Mr. Mark was happy to meet Walter but, he was creeped out when he saw Germen.

Mr. Mark said, *"Take this guy away from me, he was the only one who kidnapped me"*.

Germen felt very sad and said, *"I don't know why all the strangers are creeped out from me and I don't know if I can get my real face back again or not"*.

Katie asked everyone *"Guys, is there any way to get germen's real face back?"*.

"Yes, there is a way by which we can get his real face back" said Mr. Mark.

Germen asked Mr. Mark *"But, how?"*.

Mr. Mark answered him *"When I was ten years old, my grandfather had his own science lab in the Scarpia forest, I used to come to his lab with him in my summer vacations. He even made a chemical through which people can change their face. He used to teach me how to form the chemical composition".*

Zayden asked him *"So, do you remember the location of your grandfather's science lab?".*

Mr. Mark replied to him *"I only remember that it is located near the Maltha falls".*

XII
THE UNEXPECTED JOURNEY

Everyone went to sleep and woke up in the crack of dawn to find the Maltha falls.

Zayden asked Mr. Mark *"How far do we have to go?"*.

Mr. Mark replied to him *"Around, fifty kilometres, but it is going to be adventurous, we will be passing through difficulties"*.

Zayden shockingly replied *"What! I can't walk too far, and I can't pass through so many difficulties"*.

Mr. Mark tried explaining everyone *"Guys, try to be adventure friendly, there are times when we need to put up a fight, sometimes we need to take some risks in life"*.

Kenji asked Mr. Mark *"So, from where should we start?"*.

Mr. Mark replied, *"The lab is in the north; the Global Positioning System (GPS) is showing that we must move straight right now".*

They kept moving and moving, everyone was very tired, after walking a bit, they found a train engine on rail tracks and started to board the train engine!

Alex surprisingly said *"Yes! Now finally we will be travelling in a engine, we won't need to walk too far!!!".*

Mr. Mark told them *"Don't be too excited, we will sit in the engine for half an hour and then again we have to walk for an hour".*

They sat in the train engine, and Mr. Mark tried to start the engine but it wasn't starting!

Germen gave a suggestion *"Guys, I can try to fix the engine, I had learnt to fix the engine of any vehicle".*

It took an hour to fix the engine. They finally started the engine, everyone had brought some snacks so, everyone was eating snacks.

When ten minutes passed in the train engine, the rail was divided into two rails, but Mr. Mark didn't know that the rail was divided into two rails. When Katie was looking out of the window, she discovered that the rail was being divided into two rails!!!

Katie told everyone about it, Mr. Mark tried to turn the train, but it was too late.

Walter asked Mr. Mark *"Dad, which way did you turn and where do we need to go?".*

Mr. Mark replied to him *"Unfortunately, we needed to go towards the west, but the train is going towards the north, I couldn't turn it towards the other side"*.

Everyone was trying to figure out how to go back, while everyone was trying to figure out, Charles noticed that the railway line was ending, and the train was about to fall in a river!!!

Everyone's heart started beating, they couldn't figure out what to do. The train's engine started falling into the river, and everybody tried to hold on to something.

The engine was about to fall but, it stopped and started balancing.

Alex said, "Guys, don't move, otherwise the engine will fall down".

The engine had lost its balance and was falling, but it didn't fall!

Zayden, Katie, Alex and Kenji were surprised that why didn't the engine fall, when they looked up, they saw that Germen, Tyler, Walter, Mr. Mark and Charles were there to keep the balance, Charles was pulling them up one by one but by mistake, the engine lost its balance again!!!

The whole train engine was broken, but luckily, no one was injured, everyone was alright.

When Mr. Mark checked the Global Positioning System (GPS), he happily said *"Yes! Guys we are not that far from Maltha Falls, right now we are in the Staple River"*.

Everyone came out of the river and tried to find a way which can take them to the Maltha falls.

Going through the forest was not a good idea for them, they only had one way that was going through the Staple River.

XIII
STAPLE RIVER

None of them was willing to swim in the river. *"Guys, we can go there through a boat, if we use a boat, we will reach early, we don't need to swim,"* said Tyler.

Then Zayden said *"Yes, I like your idea, but we don't have a boat, how will we go".*

Kenji replied to him *"So, we can build a boat".*

Zayden rudely replied to him *"What! Are you crazy! We don't have any stuff through which we can build a boat and, it is a very insane path full of banyan trees".*

Kenji said, *"So what, we can search".*

Then Zayden said, *"It's very easy to say but not easy to search and build".*

Kenji tried to explain Zayden *"See, if you think that it's hard, then it will always be hard for you, and if you think that it is not going to be hard, then it will never be hard for you. Just think that you can build a boat".*

Then Zayden said believingly *"Yes, we can build a boat, but how will we make, we don't have any stuff".*

Kenji said *"Yes, we do have, we have pieces of wood, so we can join the pieces of wood with a rope and, we can cut some pieces to sail in the water".*

Then some of them brought the pieces of wood, but they didn't have a rope. They didn't have a rope; they tried a lot to find a rope.

After a long time, Charles got an idea *"Guys, we don't have a rope, so we can cut down the aerial roots from the banyan trees and use them as a rope".*

Everybody was satisfied with Charles's idea.

Everyone started cutting out the aerial roots from the banyan trees and, were attaching the pieces of wood through the aerial roots.

After an hour of making the boat, they finally started moving in the boat.

The boat was very weak, so the aerial roots got untied and all the pieces of wood separated in the water!!!

Total nine pieces of wood were used in making the boat, and each person was leaning on a piece of wood, so that they do not drown in water.

None of them knew what to do at that time.

After some time, Alex spotted a speed boat, *"Guys, there is a speed boat far away,"* said Alex.

Kenji was the closest person to the speed boat, so everyone wanted Kenji to go till the speed boat. Kenji swam till the speed boat and tried to start the boat.

He was very confused as there were many buttons in the speed boat.

He couldn't find the start button, so he randomly pressed a button, and the boat started moving very fast and left everyone else.

The speed boat was not in Kenji's control.

Kenji again pressed a button randomly, and the boat started drifting backwards.

Kenji had no idea what to do next, and after some time, he had reached far away.

The place where the speed boat was moving was very weird, Kenji felt lost.

Kenji again pressed a random button, and the boat started moving faster and he could spot boards that were showing Maltha Falls.

He again pressed a random button, and the boat finally stopped, but it stopped in front of Maltha Falls!!!

Kenji was very shocked when he reached there.

XIV

MALTHA FALLS

Kenji was very surprised to see Maltha Falls, but he didn't want to go alone, so he tried to go back to them and bring them here, but everybody reached there swimming in a while!!!

Kenji asked everyone *"Guys, why did you swim this far?"*.

Zayden replied to him *"Kenji, we didn't want to leave you alone here, so we decided to swim"*.

Mr, Mark reminded everybody *"Remember, there is a secret way of going in, try to search for it"*.

Everybody was trying to find a way to go in there. Walter went to search on the other side of the Waterfall. It was very dark on the other side of the waterfall.

Walter kept moving ahead, but still he could not find any light, so he turned on his flashlight. After 10-15 minutes, he finally reached a place full of lights.

Walter reached an empty and large place, his voice was even echoing, so he called everybody to the other side of the waterfall.

When everyone reached there, they all were very confused as it was an empty and large place.

Charles then discovered a red button on the rocks. When Charles pressed the button, an obstacle course appeared in front of them!

They even found a paper with something written on it, which said *"There are three types of obstacles which you have to cross in thirty minutes".*

Everyone started panicking as the first obstacle was in front of them. In the first obstacle, they had to go through the ropes, they had to lean on one rope and jump to the other rope.

If they leave a rope, they will fall in the waterfall!!!

No one was ready to go first except Tyler. Tyler was not at all scared, he was always ready to take risks.

He held the rope tightly and pushed himself forward and kept going forward.

Everybody was watching him, so that they can learn to do the same way. When Tyler finished it, everyone else tried crossing the same way as him. Everyone finished the first obstacle except Zayden. He was very petrified of obstacles like this one.

When everyone started encouraging him, he felt confident to try.

He finally started when he was feeling confident, he held the rope and took the same steps as Tyler. When he was holding the rope, he couldn't jump to the other rope, because his hands were sweating.

He was falling in the fall but, someone came from out of the blue and saved him!

That guy was wearing a black hoodie. Everyone was trying to see his face and then he revealed himself. When everybody saw his face, they could not believe what they saw!

That guy was Robbin!!!

Everybody was very surprised and elated to see him but confused too, because he fell in the lava.

Katie asked Robbin *"Robbin, how did you survive in the lava?"*.

Robbin explained everyone *"Guys, that lava was not real, I mean, that lava was just a kind of special effect, and I even spotted a projector, so I thought it must be Germen's job"*.

Then Germen said, *"I'm so sorry guys, I really forgot about it, I had hundreds of traps"*.

Everyone then went towards the second obstacle. In the second obstacle, they had eight ziplines, without any belts for safety, they just needed to hold it and the zipline will slide them on its own.

If anyone's grip got loose, he would fall in the fall. There were eight ziplines but there were ten people.

There was no space for the remaining two people.

After thinking about it, Walter got an idea *"Guys, eight of us can go first, and we can push back the ziplines as the distance is not too far away for the remaining two."*

So, first eight people went to the other side except Zayden and Charles.

When the eight of them reached, they pushed back the ziplines, but the ziplines stopped in between!

XV
ISSUE OF THE SECOND OBSTACLE

Everyone was left with only twenty minutes to cross the third stage.

Just then, Charles asked Zayden *"Zayden, now how will we go there, the ziplines are stuck and we don't have any other way to go to the other side".*

Zayden replied *"No, there must be a way to go to the other side".*

Zayden and Charles were trying to find a way to go the other side while, rest eight of them were trying to push the zipline towards Zayden and Charles with a stick.

While Zayden and Charles were figuring out a way to go to the other side, rest eight of them pushed the ziplines closer to them.

Both Zayden and Charles noticed that rest of them pushed the ziplines towards them, but the zipline was not too close.

Charles said *"Zayden, I think we can reach till the zipline".*

Zayden tried to explain Charles "*Charles, are you sure, because it's not too close".*

Charles said, *"Don't worry about me Zayden, I'll be okay".*

Charles jumped towards the zipline and held it tightly but, he forgot that zipline was stuck!!!

He couldn't hold it for long. His hands were sweating very badly and after a moment, he was balancing with two fingers!!!

Charles was about to fall, but Zayden quickly held the zipline and then held Charles's and saved him from falling in the waterfall.

Then Zayden was also leaning on his one and from one hand, he was holding Charles's hand so, he was trying to move forward.

"Zayden, be careful, because you are leaning on one hand," said Charles.

Zayden replied to him *"Charles, don't worry I'll be okay".*

Rest eight of them were trying to help them. They pointed a large pole towards Charles.

Charles said, *"Zayden, I will jump and hold the pole and go there".*

Zayden accepted and started the countdown *"Okay then, jump at the count of three, one....... two....... three".*

Charles caught the pole! Everyone was relieved that he could make it.

Charles reached there, and Zayden also reached there by leaning on the zipline.

Everybody went to the third and last obstacle.

In the final obstacle, there were three pieces of wood which were attached to the rope and were swinging left and right and couldn't be stopped to step on the next piece of wood and below them was the deep waterfall!

Kenji took the first step on the first piece of wood. He was unable to step on the second piece of wood.

Then, in a fluke, he jumped on the second piece! In the same way he did the third piece too.

In the same way, everyone tried to cross the obstacle.

It took ten minutes for everyone to complete. It was not too easy for them to cross it. They crossed it in the last minute!

They had finally reached the science lab!!!

They caught hold of a small book of chemicals which guided them about the recipe about how to mix the chemicals. Everyone started mixing the chemicals.

After mixing all the chemicals, Germen drank the mixture, and his face started to pain!!!

His face kept paining for 10-15 minutes and then, he finally got his real face back!!!

Everyone was very happy to see Germen's real face.

Walter wanted to give a surprise to Germen and Tyler. The surprise was their rest of the family!

In return, Germen gifted Walter all the items which are required for an explorer as he wanted to be an explorer.

From then, everyone started living happily.

Other Books By Author

He has penned a supernatural thriller 'Secret of the Den' which is his first book! The book is available on Notion Press, Amazon and Flipkart.

www.ingramcontent.com/pod-product-compliance
Lightning Source LLC
La Vergne TN
LVHW090132160826
845673LV00017B/2439

* 9 7 9 8 8 9 5 8 8 7 0 3 5 *